THE
SELECTED STORIES FROM
Jataka Tales

Compiled by
'KUNWAR' ANIL KUMAR

MANOJ PUBLICATIONS

CONTENTS

Manoj Publications

761, Main Road Burari, Delhi-110084
Phone : 27611116, 27611349
Fax : 27611546, Mobile : 9868112194
E-mail : manojpublications @ vsnl.net
Website : www.manojpublications.com
ISBN : 81-8133-410-8

Showroom :

1583-84, Dariba Kalan,
Chandani Chowk, Delhi-6
Phone : 23262174, 23268216
Mobile : 9818753569

Printers :
Jain Offset Printers

REAL DISCIPLE

PANDIT Ramnarain was the greatest scholar of his time. He was respected by all.

He had his Ashram in a jungle outside Kanchanpur. Students from far-off places came to him to get education.

Panditji never observed any difference among his students. Be it son of a king or that of a beggar; everyone was imparted education without any discrimination.

Panditji had a daughter. She was his only issue, and was moving towards adolescence very fast. Panditji wanted to get her married as soon as possible and fulfil his duty.

His daughter was very affable, gentle and wise. Panditji was looking for a just as affable, gentle and wise boy for her.

One day, an idea of putting all his disciples to test, flashed across the mind of Panditji. He decided that he will give his daughter's hand in marriage to the most suitable one.

Next day Panditji called all his disciples and said, "My children! I am in a very difficult situation."

"What kind of difficult situation is it, sir," asked a young boy whose name was Bhimsen.

"In fact, my daughter has become marriageable, and I have never saved anything for this purpose. Now I have decided to get her married at an early date and I shall be needing clothes and ornaments for her."

"No need to be worried about," said a handsome young boy. "You only have to wish and I shall offer thousands of gold coins at your feet. My father is the wealthiest person of the town.

"No, no, sir! I shall feel greatly obliged If I am given a chance. I am the prince of this kingdom. Just make a hint and I shall bring heaps of diamonds, pearls, gold and silver at your feet.

Thus, many young boys came forward with their offers according to their capability. But Panditji did not accept anyone's offer and said, "No, no, I shall have lost my prestige in this manner. People will say that Panditji has stooped to begging to get his daughter married."

"In that case, sir, you please suggest some way yourself. Tell us, in what way we can solve your problem," Prince Veersingh said.

"My children! you have to do something that may serve my purpuse without jeopardizing my status of a Guru. So, I suggest to you all to commit thefts and bring the required things little by little; but remember one thing—no one should know about it; if your right hand is involved in thievery, your left hand should not know about it. It should be a top secret."

"Please do not worry, sir!" said all the disciples in unison. "Your orders will be carried out."

And then the group of the disciples dispersed in all directions in order to carry out the orders of their Guru.

Whichever disciple brought clothes or ornaments, quietly handed it over to Guruji.

In a few days, Guruji had lots of clothes and ornaments accumulated in his Ashram.

Guruji was carefully keeping thing's separately, brought by each of his disciples. After a few days, Guruji noticed that almost every disciple except Bhimsen had brought something or the other. Bhimsen had not yet stolen anything for Guruji.

So, one day, Guruji gathered all his disciples and said, "Bhimsen, every disciple of mine has stolen something for me according to his capability, but so many days have passed, and I find that you have not stolen anything for me. Is it that you don't want to help me reduce my stress and worry?"

"I do want Gurudev," said Bhimsen humbly.

"Then why is it that you did not steal anything for me?"

"How could I do that, Gurudev? Your orders were such that it always checked me from doing so," said Bhimsen.

"What do you mean?" Panditji looked at him with sharp eyes.

The other disciples were dumbfounded. Guruji had himself asked us to commit thefts; then what kind of orders was he talking about?

"Guruji!" Bhimsen said, "You had yourself instructed us to commit thefts, but it was with a precondition that no one should know about it. Even if our right hand was involved in thievery, our left hand should not know about it.

"Yes, I had said that, but what was the problem?"

"Guruji! You have yourself taught us that there isn't anything that is hidden from our souls. In that case, how could I have kept a secret of it from my soul? This is the only reason why I could not steal anything till today."

"You are great, my son!" Pandit Ramnarain patted his back and praised him. He embraced him and said, "Bhimsen! You are my real disciple." Then turning towards other disciples, he said, "Look, my children! I am very happy that all of you are very obedient and you have obeyed me, taking all sorts of risks; but, my children! remember one thing—if your parents, your brothers and sisters or even if your Guru asks you to do something wrong, you should refuse to do it. Never do anything wrong in your life. I had staged this scene to put you all to test and also to find a suitable boy for my daughter's marriage. And now I am proud to declare that Bhimsen is the most suitable boy for my daughter."

"I am sure you must have learnt a new lesson. Now please go and return all the things that you have stolen, to their owners."

"Guruji, we admit that Bhimsen is the worthiest of all of us. We accept him as the son-in-law of our Guru." Saying this all the disciples lifted Bhimsen on their shoulders and began dancing.

A strange fair used to be organised every year in Vijayapur state. It was strange because it used to be a fair of rams. The villagers of the neighbouring villages used to collect in the fair with their stout rams, arrange a fight between two rams and enjoy the scene.

This year also a fair of rams had been organised. There was a big crowd of thousands in the main market of the town. So, many farmers had brought at least one stout ram each with them. Just as a fight of rams was going to be organised, a saint happened to arrive at that place, and seeing a big gathering he enquired about the occasion and the reason behind such a big gathering.

One of the farmers explained to him—"Maharaj! this is a fair of rams, and it is organised here every year. So many groups of two rams each is made and they are made to fight between them. The winning ram in the finals is declared the king of rams, and the owner of the winning ram is awarded lots of prizes."

"Is that so?" said the saint with surprise and making his way through the crowd. He came forward and stood right before the arena to have a clearer view.

The fight had started and everyone was watching it with fun. Suddenly one of the fighting rams stopped and began looking at the saint with his gaze fixed on him. The other ram also stopped.

The ram came and stood before the saint. It recoiled a few paces with its head down, ready to charge at him.

But the saint thought, "Ah, here is a good and intelligent animal. He has realised that I am a man of merit, and he is bowing to give me a salute. At least he knows how to honour a saint."

The owner of the ram was quick to realise that the saint was feeling flattered, so in a bid to alert him, he said, "Maharaj! Please get out of its way or else it will hit you. Don't think that this ram in bowing before you in a gesture of salute; it is preparing itself to launch an attack on you. Be careful, please!"

"No, no, come on! This is a spechless creature. How will it hit anyone. It, in fact, wants to have my blessings. It is us human beings who torture these spechless creature."

"Maharaj! You are forgetting that it's a ram and is violent by nature. Even God cannot change its nature. It is the individual nature of every creature in the world that tells about it."

"No, no, you are a fool!"

Another person standing near him, said, "Maharaj! These rams are meant for fighting. Violence is there in their nature."

But the saint didn't listen to anyone. On the contrary, he advanced towards the ram, and the ram also advanced two paces towards the saint. The owner of the ram tried to stop the ram, but by that time it was too late.

And in the twinkling of an eye, the ram took the saint on its horns and sent him rolling to the ground.

"Hey, Ram!" The saint shrieked with pain.

The saint fell face down on the ground and broke all his teeth. His mouth filled with blood.

People around somehow managed to push the ram back and helping the saint stand on his feet, they said, "Why, Maharaj! Had we not told you that rams are violent by nature?"

"Yes, brothers!" said the saint whining with pain—"It was indeed my mistake. You were right when you said that rams are violent by nature. Oh, God! It has broken my bones."

Poeple pulled the saint back and gave him some water to clean his mouth. The saint took water in his mouth and kept squirting it out until his mouth became clean. Then he was offered some milk to drink. Now it had become clear to the saint that every creature has its own individual nature.

DECIDING THE SHARE

THERE lived a pair of male and female jackals in a forest. They loved each other very much. The male jackal loved the female jackal so much that he would fulfil every demand made by her. One day the female jackal said, "Dear! I have a great urge for eating fish today."

"That's no problem. I shall bring fish for you, If you have an urge for it, dear."

Saying this he set out in search of fish

While going towards the river, he began thinking—'I have promised my wife to arrange fish for her, but I know nothing about fishing. How to fulfil my wife's demand for fish?'

Lost in these thoughts the jackal reached the bank of the river and sitting in a corner he began looking at the frolicking fish with greedy eyes. For once he felt like jumping into the river and getting the required fish in the twinkling of an eye. But seeing water all around in the big river, and the water current, frightened him. He got so scared to see the vast river that he went away from the river-bank and sat under a tree at quite a distance. He began thinking of some possible ruse to get the fish without risking his life.

Just then he saw an otter bringing a big fish out of the river with the help of his friends. One otter said to the other—"This is a very big fish. We can manage our meals with this fish for days together."

"Yes, brother! This is after a very long time that we have fished such a big one."

"The jackal's mouth began watering to see that fish. He began thinking how to get it from their possession. He thought—'Using my wits I can manage to get the fish in my possession.'

The otters somehow pull led the fish to the bank of the river. One of the otters said, "Friend! we have got only one fish between us; and we are two. How to decide our shares!"

"Let us do it ourselves," said the other one.

"Look, brother!" said the first one, "Deciding the shares ourselves will give a rise to doubt in our minds, and both of us will keep thinking that the other one may have taken a larger share. So, this is my sincere advice that we get the shares decided by someone who is not one of us; a third one."

The jackal became very happy to hear this. He came forward like an elderly person and said, "Brother! What's your problem?"

"Not a big problem," said one otter, "In fact, we both of us have killed this big fish. We are two and we have got only one fish between us. Now the problem is how to decide our shares."

"This can be done by someone who is not one of us," said the other otter.

"What you say is correct, brother. Look, if you want I can help you. I take pleasure in solving the problems of others. If you wish I can bring out an amicable solution to your dispute."

"All right, brother! I have no objection, provided he too doesn't have any objections," said one otter.

"I too, have no objection, brother."

"That's great! This is called friendship. A peaceful agreement solves many big problems. We should always share our meals together; we must trust each other; there isn't anything greater than love and affection in this world. Both of you please wait for me here. I shall go and bring a knife from somewhere, so that it becomes easy to cut the fish and decide your shares."

"Yes, yes, brother! Please go and bring a knife. We shall wait for you here."

While coming towards the river, the jackal had seen a farmer lying in his cot and guarding his farm. He had also seen a wooden staff and a big knife on his cot. He was sleeping when the jackal reached there. He quietly picked up the knife and returned with it.

Both the otters saw him returning with a big knife happily.

16

"Come brothers! Now I can help you solve your problem."
Saying this the jackal cut the fish into three pieces. First he cut the head off and then the tail.

"Brother! You take the top portion of the fish—the head; and you take the bottom portion—the tail."

Both took their shares, and now they had their eyes fixed on the middle portion of the fish. Both were thinking that the jackal would divide it also into two halves and give them their shares.

But the jackal took the third piece in his possession.

"Brother! Will you not divide the remaining piece?"

"This piece should not concern you, brother," said the jackal looking at them with angry eyes. "This is for the job done by me. Will you not pay me for the pains taken by me in going all the way to get a knife and decide your shares for you? The fruits of hard work should be shared by all. After all I too am your friend.

Saying this the jackal took the middle portion of the fish in his mouth and went away. Both the otters were left behind to see him go with the largest of the three pieces of the fish. And by the time they realised what had actually happened, it was too late.

"Brother! How much better it would have been, if we had decided our shares ourselves. Now see! He gave us the top and the bottom portions of the fish in our shares and went away with the largest piece in his mouth."

The other otter said, "Someone has correctly said that a dispute between two friends always benefits the third one. Now let us take a lesson from this event that a marginal difference in our share would not bother us, and we shall never allow anyone to mediate between us."

THREE CUNNING BROTHERS

THERE lived three brothers in a village. They had remarkable deftness in fabricating stories. There stories used to be full of impossible events. Once these three brothers set out on a journey. When the sun set, and it started becoming dark and they were still half way to go, they decided to halt in an inn. A prince had also halted there. He was wearing expensive garments studded with gems and diamonds.

These brothers had never seen a prince; so seeing the prince they became very jealous of him. They thought why not make a fool of the prince also by fabricating some impossible stories.

They came to the prince and said, "Wouldn't it be nice for all of us to tell one story each and make the evening enjoyable?"

The prince liked this idea.

Immediately one of the brothers said, "Anyone of us who doesn't believe the story told by any of us, will become slave of the one who was telling the story."

They selected and made an elderly person of the inn, a judge in order to announce his judgement in the event of disagreement on any point. They were confident that hearing their fabricated stories, full of impossible events, the prince will definitely express his disbelief, and either he will agree to become their slave or, in order to avoid becoming a slave, he will give some valuable things to them as penalty.

Some others, staying in the inn, also joined them, and sat around them to enjoy hearing stories. The eldest brother stood and began telling his story—"When I was very young, I was very fond of playing the game of 'thief and police.' One day, while playing, I climbed a tall tree and hid myself in it. My brothers began searching for me. They kept looking around but couldn't find me. When it began getting dark, they gave up and returned disappointed. Now the problem before me was that I had to climb down, and by now it had become so dark that I could hardly see anything. So, I went to a nearby village and brought a rope from a hut. With the help of the rope I managed to come down without any problem and returned home safely."

The prince heard this baseless story. He simply smiled and began waiting for the other one to start. The other two brothers were surprised that the prince had easily believed their eldest brother's story and didn't raise any question.

Anyway...the second brother began telling his story—

"That evening, when we were searching for our brother, who was hiding in a tree, I heard the rustle of something moving furtively in the bushes. I thought my brother was hiding there. I rushed in that direction, but surprisingly a dangerous and hungry lion appeared from behind the bushes. He had hardly opened his jaws when I dived into his mouth with lightning speed. I did all this at such a great speed that the lion could not get a chance to chew me. I had entered his stomach unscathed. Now I began jumping around, and I created so much problem for him that the lion began weeping with pain. Ultimately, in order to get rid of me, the lion regurgitated me, and that too with so much power that I was catapulted to my village, some two hundred miles away from there.

I dusted myself and stood erect, as if nothing had happened to me. Thus I saved the villagers from that lion. And the lion was so frightened that he never dared come to that village ever in his life."

Hearing this story also, the prince didn't say anything. He began looking at the third brother with a smile, waiting for him also to start telling his story.

The third brother was stunned to see how the prince had digested a story beyond logic. He began telling his story hesitatingly—"One day I was taking a stroll along the bank of a river. I saw that all the fishermen were looking towards the river with disappointment. When I enquired about their plight, they said that they hadn't been able to catch a single fish during the entire week. Since they had not been able to earn a single penny, their family members were starving. I decided to help them and dived into the river. Apart from helping them I also wanted to know why these fishermen had not been able to catch a single fish in seven days.

I had hardly gone a little distance towards the bed of the river when I saw a giant fish moving freely and looking for its prey. And the small fish were trying to hide themselves in different corners of the river. Now I understood why these poor fishermen had not been able to catch any fish during this period. This gaint fish had eaten away a majority of fish in the river. I immediately transformed myself into a fish and began advancing towards the giant fish. The giant fish began chasing me, and in this process she reached near the bank of the river. The fishermen were already waiting there for this fish with long spears in their hands. All of them attacked the fish and killed it. I was happy that I was able to help them and that their families won't starve any more. I transformed myself back into human form. All the fishermen and the villagers became very happy with me and they bid me farewell with lots of very costly gifts."

All the three brothers got very nonplussed to see that the prince had remained absolutely indifferent even after hearing the third story which was also full of impossible events. So, cunning as they were, these three brothers signalled to each other silently that they too would remain indifferent and won't make any queries no matter how unbelievable the story of the prince may be.

The prince started his story thus—

"I am a prince. There is no end to my property. I have come out in search of all the three slaves of mine who have suddenly absconded from my palace. I was also very fond of those three slaves, and that's the reason why I have been wandering in search of them. In a way I had lost all my hopes, but accidently I happened to meet them today. And now my search has come to an end, as fortunately I have been able to get my slaves back. And do you know who those slaves are? You three brothers!"

Hearing the story of the prince they were overcome by a kind of stupor. They were trapped in their own trickery. Now the situation was that if they refused to believe his story, they would lose, and even believing the story would make them his slaves.

Then the judge announced his judgement in favour of the prince and declared that he had won the bet, and that it was incumbent on the three brothers to accept his slavery.

The prince had a hearty laugh to see them in this funny situation. He freed these cunning brothers on condition that in future they should not try to trap simple and innocent people in their fabricated and unbelievable stories.

The three brothers promised to restrain themselves from such activities, and thus saved their lives from slavery.

From that day onwards none heard these brothers telling false and baseless stories.

NATURAL BALANCE

ONCE a saint was touring different places with his disciples. One day, wandering with his disciples, he reached a village. Since the sun had set and it was getting dark, he went to the shop of a blacksmith and requested him to allow them some place where they could sleep in the night. The blacksmith extended wholehearted hospitality to the saint and his disciples. He offered them meals and gave them sufficient place to sleep in his house. He said to the saint, "Lord! I beg your forgiveness if there has been any inconvenience to any of you in my house."

The saint said, "My son! We are very happy with your hospitality, and I grant you three boons. You may ask for anything."

First the blacksmith hesitated and then said, "Lord! If you do wish to give me something, kindly grant me a life of hundred years."

"So be it!" said the saint. "Now what's your second wish?"

The blacksmith was always worried about getting business orders. So, he wished that there should be no dearth of it.

The saint granted him the second boon also, and asked him to make his third wish.

The blacksmith could not immediately think of anything to make his third wish. So, he said, "Lord! Anyone who sits in this chair, in which you are sitting, should get stuck to it, and should not be able to leave it, unless desired by me."

The saint said, "So be it!" and left with his disciples.

The boons of the saint came true one by one. The friends and relatives of the blacksmith died one after the other in due course of time, but the blacksmith remained as healthy as ever. He also had no scarcity of business orders. He used to sing all day and do his work happily. But no one on earth is immortal. Everyone has his final day. The blacksmith also completed his hundred years, and the final day arrived. The god of death came and asked to go with him. First the blacksmith became very nervous, but then he said, "You are welcome, O Lord of Death! Please sit in this chair. Meanwhile, allow me to arrange my tools in proper order."

As soon as the god of death sat in the chair, the blacksmith roared into laughter and said, "Now you are stuck to the chair and cannot leave it without my permission."

The god of death began wriggling about in the chair, but could not free himself. The blacksmith left him there and went away giggling about his awkward situation.

Thinking that the god of death was in his captivity, the blacksmith became very happy. He thought of having a nice meal. He decided to cook chicken for himself. But as soon as he beheaded the chicken, the neck of the chicken automatically got fixed in its body; it returned to its original form and fluttered away.

The blacksmith ran after the chicken but could not catch it. Then he slaughtered a goat, but surprisingly the goat also returned to its original form and ran away. Now the blacksmith understood the mystery behind the sequence of happenings. He struck his forehead with his hand and said, "What a fool am I? When the god of death is in my captivity, how can anyone die? Well! Not bad! At least there won't be unpleasantness of death on the earth any more. I can manage with vegetarian meals, but at least my life will be secured." But by the end of the year the whole world began facing great difficulties. Because no human beings, no animals, no birds, and no insects died, and the number of creatures began increasing. Millions and millions of mosquitoes, flies, insects, rats, and frogs were born, but none died. These creatures began causing harm to farms also.

The birds ate all the fruits of the trees. The rivers and oceans became so full of fish, frogs, and other creatures that the water began stinking, and it was no more potable.

The sky looked black with locusts and mosquitoes flying all around. Dreadful snakes and wild beasts were loitering freely. Nature had lost its balance. Now everyone was in trouble. There was complete chaos all over.

Seeing such imbalance, the blacksmith realised his mistake. Now he realised that nature was incomplete without death; death was essential for keeping the nature in perfect balance.

The blacksmith came home in great speed and freed the god of death. The god of death fastened his noose around his neck and took him away with him.

After that everything became normal gradually. Creatures began dying and the nature began retrieving its balance.

TIT FOR TAT

There lived a camel in a village. Everyday he used to go to a nearby lush farm to graze. The camel was very simple and honest. There was a jackal who was his friend and was very cunning and crafty. Often he used to ride the camel and at times he used to create problems also for him. But since the camel had never undergone any major problem, he generally ignored his misdeeds.

One day the jackal said to him, "Brother camel! There is a big farm nearby; and I have seen big and tasty cucumbers in it. Let us go and eat them. For the last so many days I have been eating very ordinary and tasteless stuff, and I am tired of it. This will bring some change."

Cunning as he was, the jackal gave such a description of the cucumbers that the camel's mouth began watering with an immense desire to eat them, and he became so restless that he immediately set out to the farm. After reaching the farm the jackal began eating cucumbers; and since jackals are small in size, he had assuaged his hunger very soon. But the camel had hardly eaten anything. Meanwhile, since the jackal had already eaten his fill, he began howling loudly without caring for the camel. The camel tried to restrain the jackal from doing so, but he wouldn't listen to him. He said, "What can I do, brother camel? I am help- less. Howling after eating something is a must for me. If I don't, I start feeling very uneasy," saying this, he began howling again.

Hearing a jackal howling, the owner of the farm came running to his farm with a big stick in his hand. The jackal saw him coming. Because of his small size, he managed to escape through bushes without being noticed. But poor camel, though he also tried to escape, was caught and beaten mercilessly.

This happening made the camel so angry that he stopped talking to the jackal. The jackal also didn't come to see him for many days; but he had thoroughly enjoyed seeing the camel being beaten by the farm owner. As if this was not enough, he was looking for another such opportunity to get him thrashed again.

One day the jackal met the camel and said very humbly, "Brother! I am indeed very sorry for the happening on that day, and I sincerely apologize. In fact, the problem with me is that I am used to howling after eating anything. But please forget the past and let us make a new beginning. Come with me to enjoy the taste of tasty cucumbers. I promise that I shall not howl this time. Come with me and enjoy eating your fill. This time we are not going to that old farm. I have seen a farm across the river; we shall go there."

The poor camel was very simple and innocent. Once again the jackal managed to coax him and go across the river to eat cucumbers. And once again the jackal ate his fill quickly and returned to his old habit of howling. The guard of the farm heard him howling and came running with a big stick in his hand. The jackal took advantage of his small size and disappeared from the scene. But poor camel was trapped! He could not make his escape. And the result was that the camel was once again beaten thoroughly.

The camel was badly injured and he decided, much against his nature, that he would teach the wretched jackal a lesson. So, while on their return, the jackal was riding his back as usual and the camel was crossing the river and was in midstream, an idea suddenly flashed across his mind. He began weltering and rolling.

"Brother camel! What are you doing? I shall get drowned. Don't do this to me please," said the jackal nervously.

"Brother! Whether you drown or survive; I am not bothered about it. The problem with me is that when I see water after being beaten, I get an impulse to roll and toss about in waves." Saying this the camel began rolling on his back in the river. And the wretched jackal was taken away by the restless waves of the river. Thus, the jackal got what he rightly deserved.

BAD DEEDS BAD END

THERE lived a weaver in a village. He had two wives. He had one daughter each from both of them. Elder wife's daughter's name was Sukkhu and the younger wife's daughter's name was Dukkhu. According to her name, Sukkhu lived with her mother happily, because the weaver loved his elder wife and her daughter very much. Whereas Dukkhu and her mother were in an extreme state of distress, because the weaver never cared for them. Both, mother and daughter were humble and kind. They would remain busy in the household work from dawn to dusk, but would never complain about it.

One day the weaver died due to heart failure. After his death, Sukkhu's mother misappropriated all the property with great ingenuity and kicked them out of the house. Now Dukkhu and her mother would weave cloth whole day and somehow manage their bread and butter with the money they would get by selling it. On the contrary Sukkhu and her mother were passing their days happily and spending lavishly. Even then Sukkhu's mother was not satisfied. Day and night she used to keep planning to do some harm to Dukkhu's mother.

But she had not yet had an opportunity to do so. So many times she made plans, tried to execute them, but every time, by sheer providence, Dukkhu's mother escaped her ill designs.

One day Dukkhu's mother left some cotton outside in the sun for drying, and telling her daughter to keep a watch, she herself went to a nearby pond to fetch some water. Suddenly wind began blowing in sharp gusts, and before Dukkhu could understand anything or do anything, it took away all the cotton with itself. Dukkhu tried to collect the cotton but in vain. At last she gave up and began weeping bitterly. The god of wind saw her weeping and felt pity on her.

He materialized before her and began consoling her. He said, "Dukkhu! you follow me; I shall have your cotton retrieved."

Dejected Dukkhu met a cow in the way. The cow requested her to clean the cow dung around her, and feed her green grass. Dukkhu did it and left the place.

She had gone only a few steps when a banana tree stopped her and requested her to clean the dirt around. Having cleaned the dirt she had hardly gone a few steps when a horse stopped her, and requested her to get him some grass and water.

Having satisfied everyone, she moved forward. She saw an old lady with white hair, deeply engrossed in spinning yarn. And miraculously the spinned yarn was automatically getting converted into beautiful sarees.

The god of wind told Dukkhu that the old lady was Moon's mother. He also told her to ask the old lady for her cotton.

When Dukkhu touched the old mother's feet humbly and asked for her cotton, she blessed her and said, "My sweet daughter! First go, take a bath and eat something. There is a towel in the front room, there are some sarees in another room; you can take any saree you like. There is some hair oil in the third room; put it in your hair and take a dip in the pond which is behind my house. And then I shall return your cotton."

As ordered by the old mother, Dukkhu took a towel and went in the other room; she was simply dumbstruck to see so many expensive sarees there; but she chose the simplest one for herself, and the oil she selected to put in her hair, too, was of a very ordinary type. She set out to the pond.

Just as she had taken a dip in the pond, she was transformed into a beautiful fairy. But as there was no mirror around, she could not become aware of the development. She took one more dip and there was another miracle. Now she was heavily laden with expensive and beautiful ornaments. She was frightened to see this miracle, and could not dare take another dip. She came out of the pond and went straight to the old mother.

The old mother asked her to go to the dining room to have her meals. There were different kinds of dainty dishes. But Dukkhu was a different kind of girl. Despite being poor, she was not greedy. She took simple food and that too in a very little quantity, and assuaged her hunger. The old mother gently caressed her hair and said, "Go, my daughter! Go to the fourth room. There are many small boxes filled with cotton. You can take any box you like."

Dukkhu went to the fourth room and thinking that she was a poor girl and she should take a thing that suited her status, she took the smallest box and came back to the old mother. She took her blessings and set out to her home.

While she was on the way to her home, the horse gave her a pitcher full of gold coins, the banana tree gave her a compact pendent bunch of golden banana, and the cow gave her a young cow who could be milked any time. Now Dukkhu wanted to reach home with all those gifts at the earliest. She knew her mother must be getting worried to find her missing.

Dukkhu reached home after some time and called her mother. Dukkhu's mother came running, but was stunned to see her completely transformed.

After hearing the whole sequence of happenings, Dukkhu's mother thanked God and said, "Oh, my darling! My sweet daughter! it's nothing but God's grace."

Dukkhu's mother went to Sukkhu's mother and very humbly, she offered to share the gifts. But Sukkhu's mother was filled with jealousy and refused to share the gifts straightaway.

Feeling greatly insulted, Dukkhu and her mother returned home. They opened the box of cotton in the night. But instead of cotton they saw a very handsome prince coming out of the box. They were simply overwhelmed to see him. The prince married Dukkhu and all the three began living happily.

Seeing this Sukkhu's jealous mother also planned to send her daughter to the old mother. She, in a bid to follow the exact sequence of happenings, kept some cotton outside for drying. Suddenly gusts of wind took away her cotton also, and the god of wind asked Sukkhu to follow him.

Sukkhu began following him in great speed. The cow, the banana tree, and the horse tried to stop her in the way, asking for the same favours; but she gave them a disdainful look, and continued moving in the same speed.

She did not even care to wish when she saw the old mother, and asked her to give her also the box of cotton in gift. The old mother listened to her patiently, and asked her also to do things that she had asked Dukkhu to do. And Sukkhu in all her greediness, selected the costliest Saree for herself; then she put scented oil in her hair, and taking a big mirror, went to take dips in the pond. She closed her eyes and within moments she took three to four dips in the pond. But when she posed before the mirror to see her image, she was terribly frightened. She was horrified to see herself in such a form.

She looked ugly like an ogress. She screamed with fear and went running to the old mother. The old mother said, "This is all due to your greediness. You forgot my instructions and in a hurry you took two extra dips.

Then she asked Sukkhu to forget about it and directed her to go to the dining hall. There too, her greedy nature made her select the daintiest dishes for eating.

Having eaten gluttonously she belched in a very ugly manner and went straight to the room where boxes full of cotton were kept. She selected the biggest box and left the place without even saying good-bye to the old mother, and set out to her home muttering inaudibly.

In the way, the horse kicked her, the banana tree dropped a heavy bunch of bananas on her head, and the cow chased her with her pointed hornes. Somehow, saving herself from all these, she managed to reach home. She was weeping bitterly. But the worse came to worst when her own mother refused to recognize her.

But when Sukkhu narrated her sad story, her dejected mother took it as her ill fate; she didn't say anything. Only one thing was left as hope, and that was the box filled with cotton. Her greedy mother suggested to her to open the box at night in isolation. When it became absolutely dark, she left Sukkhu alone in a room, bolted the door from outside and went to sleep.

Next day she kept waiting for her daughter, expecting her to come out of the room with a handsome prince. She unlatched the door from outside and began knocking at it. But when the door didn't open for a long time, she became very nervous. She took an axe and broke the door. The scene inside the room was ghastly.

What she saw was the skeleton of her daughter on one side, and a slough of a big python on the other. In a corner there was the box of cotton lying open.

Sukkhu's mother had been punished by nature for her bad deeds. Now she had no alternative except to weep and repent. That's why it is said that bad deeds have bad ends.